WELCOME TO
PASSPORT TO READING
A beginning reader's ticket to a brand-new world!

Every book in this program is designed to build read-along and read-alone skills, level by level, through engaging and enriching stories. As the reader turns each page, he or she will become more confident with new vocabulary, sight words, and comprehension.

These PASSPORT TO READING levels will help you choose the perfect book for every reader.

READING TOGETHER
Read short words in simple sentence structures together to begin a reader's journey.

READING OUT LOUD
Encourage developing readers to sound out words in more complex stories with simple vocabulary.

READING INDEPENDENTLY
Newly independent readers gain confidence reading more complex sentences with higher word counts.

READY TO READ MORE
Readers prepare for chapter books with fewer illustrations and longer paragraphs.

This book features sight words from the educator-supported Dolch Sight Word List. Readers will become more familiar with these commonly used vocabulary words, increasing reading speed and fluency.

For more information, please visit www.passporttoreadingbooks.com, where each reader can add stamps to a personalized passport while traveling through story after story!

Enjoy the journey!

Little, Brown and Company

Hachette Book Group
237 Park Avenue, New York, NY 10017
Visit our website at www.lb-kids.com

LB kids is an imprint of Little, Brown and Company. The LB kids name and logo
are trademarks of Hachette Book Group, Inc.

The publisher is not responsible for websites (or their content)
that are not owned by the publisher.

First Edition: September 2011

ISBN: 978-0-316-17629-3

Library of Congress Control Number: 2011926081

10 9 8 7 6 5 4 3 2 1

CW

Printed in the United States of America

MARVEL SUPER HERO SQUAD™

TEAM SPIRIT!

by Lucy Rosen
illustrated by Dario Brizuela

LITTLE, BROWN & COMPANY
LB kids

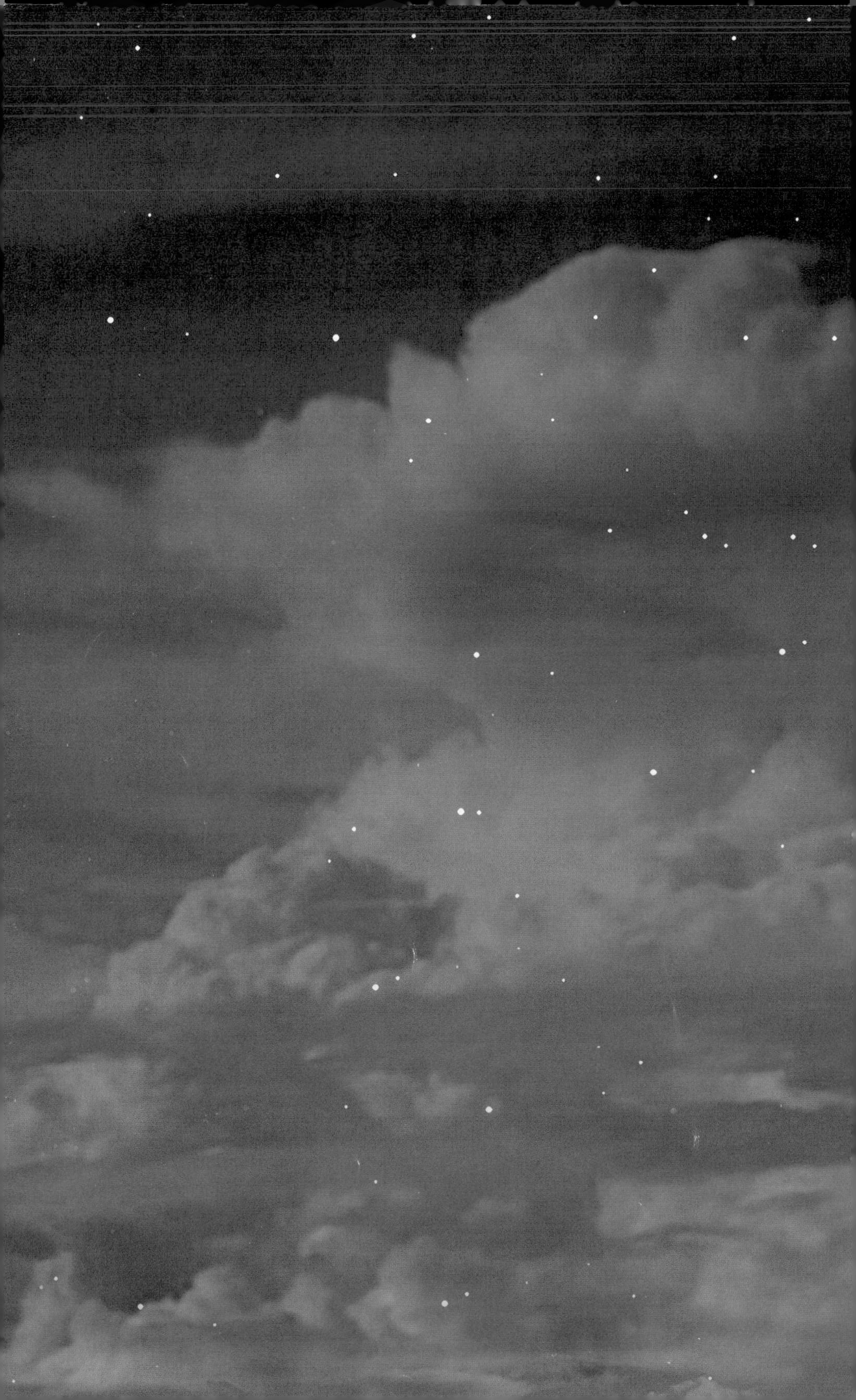

Attention,

all Super Hero Squad fans!

Look for these items when you read this book.

Can you spot them all?

SENTINEL

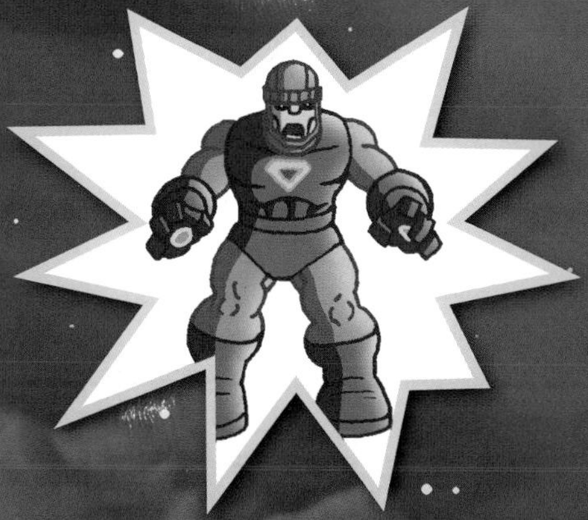

STATUE

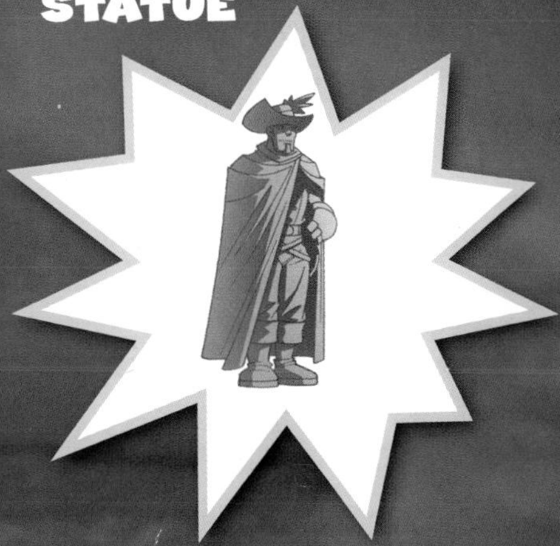

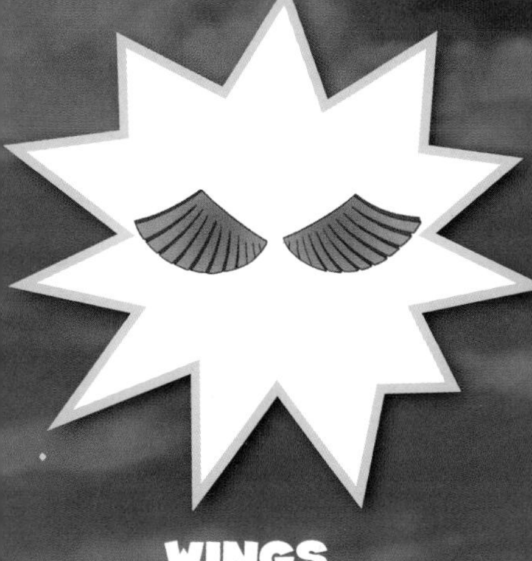

WINGS

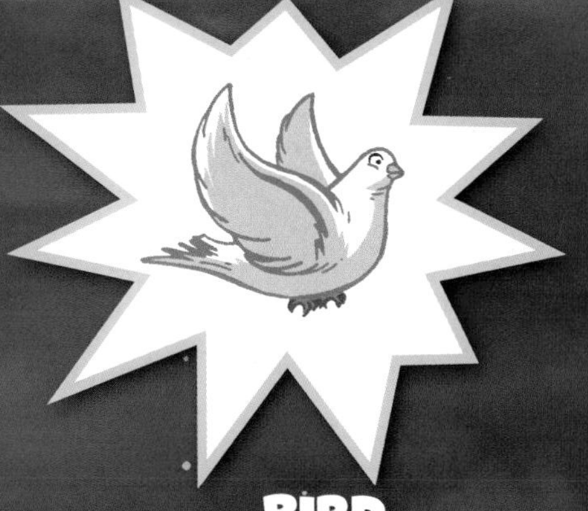

BIRD

Wolverine, Storm, and Spider-Man
have just come back from a mission.

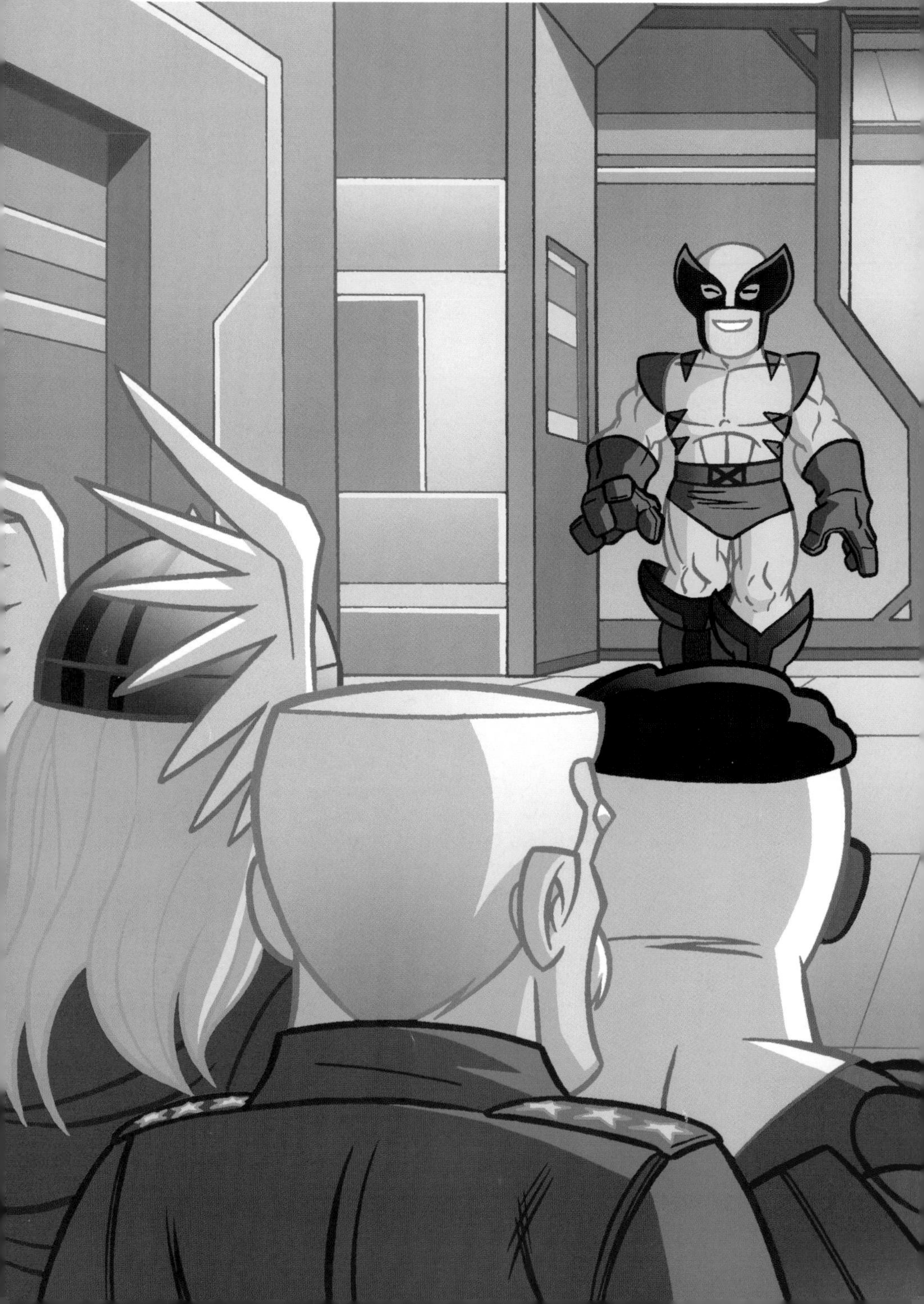

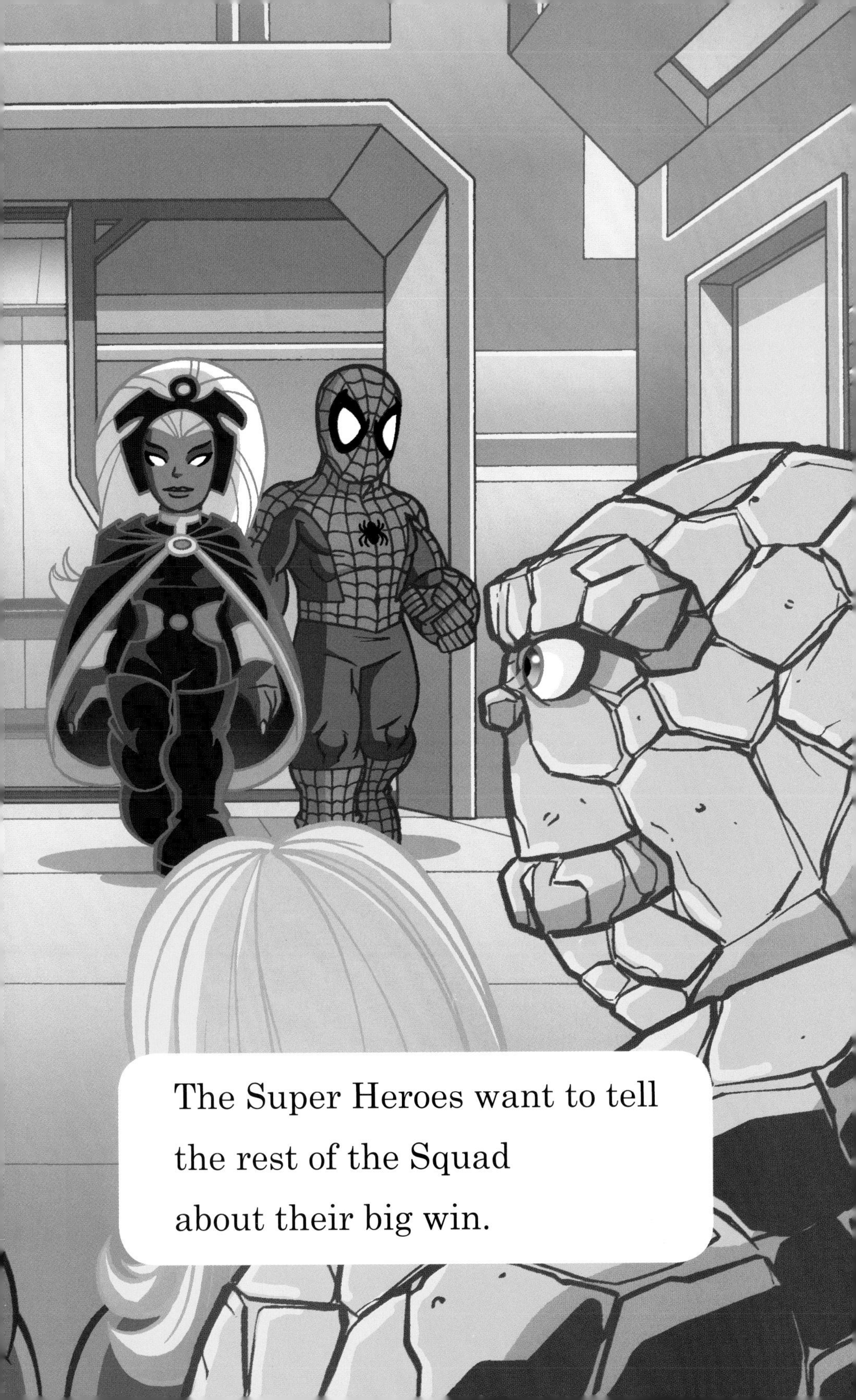

The Super Heroes want to tell
the rest of the Squad
about their big win.

"We hid in my fog cloud," says Storm,
"to sneak into Dr. Doom's place.
Spider-Man used his web
to pull down the gate."

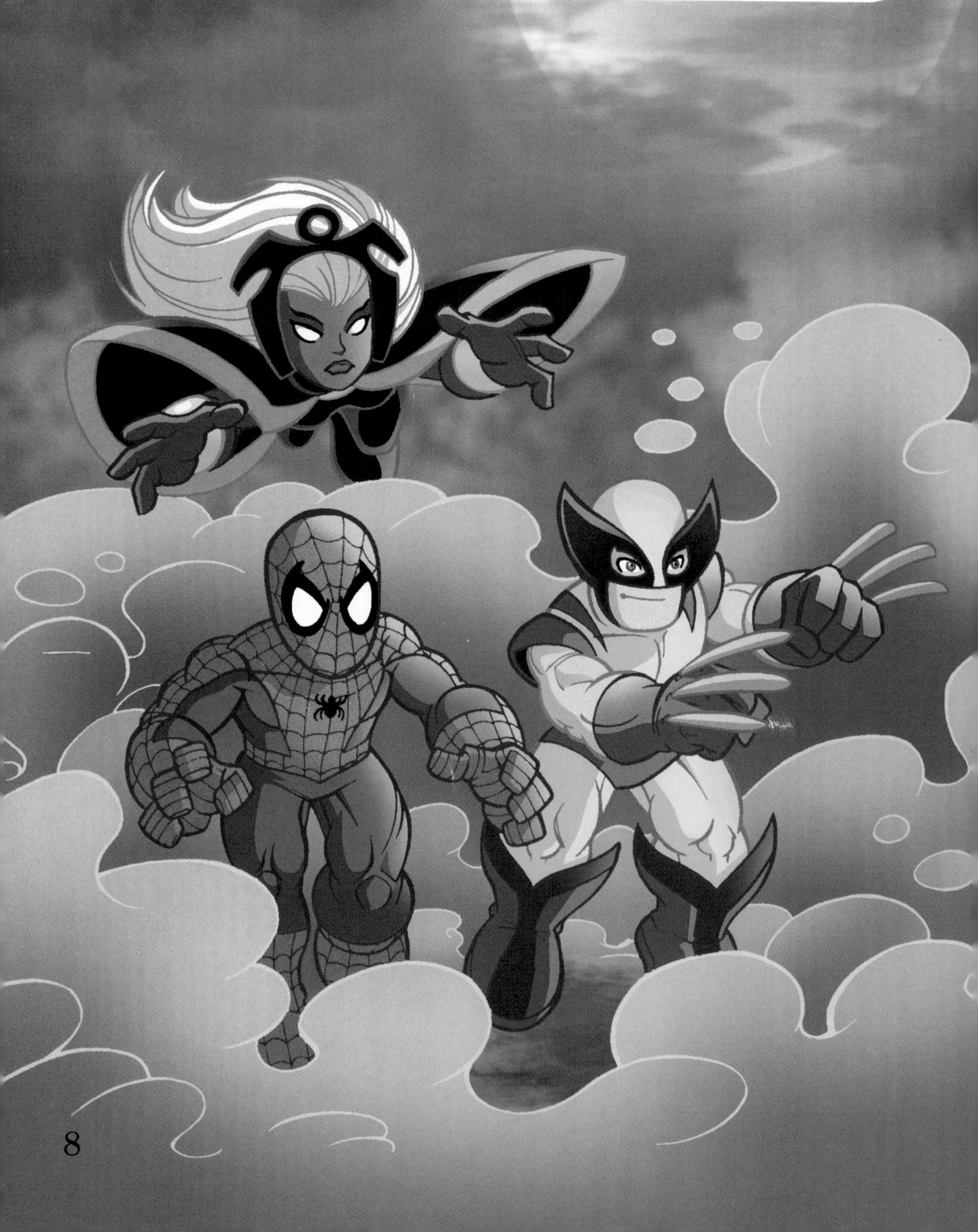

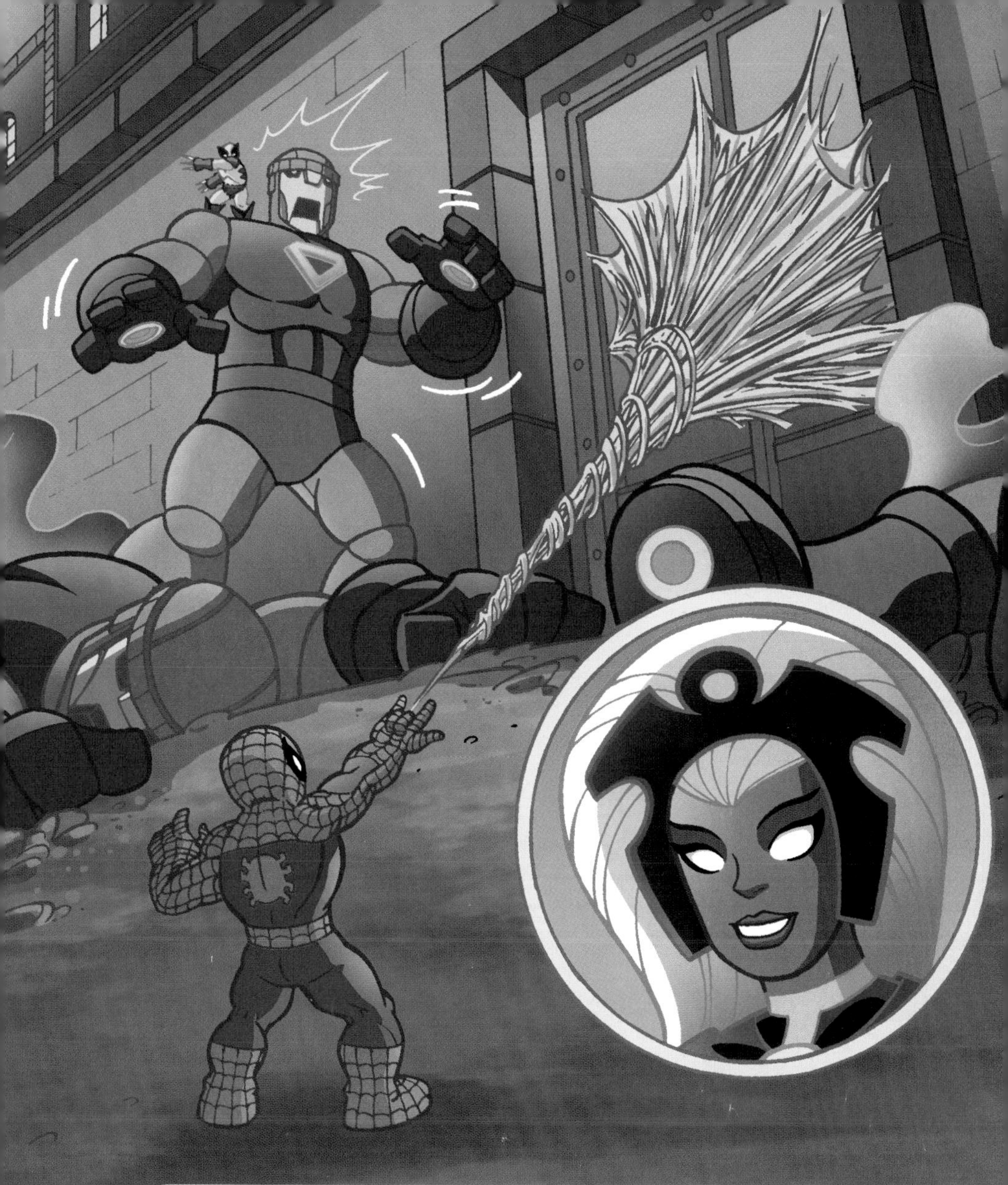

"Then Wolverine used his claws to shut down the Sentinels. The villains never even knew we were there!"

"Wow," says Invisible Woman.
"That sounds . . . amazing."
"And a lot like their last three *amazing* adventures," says Thing.

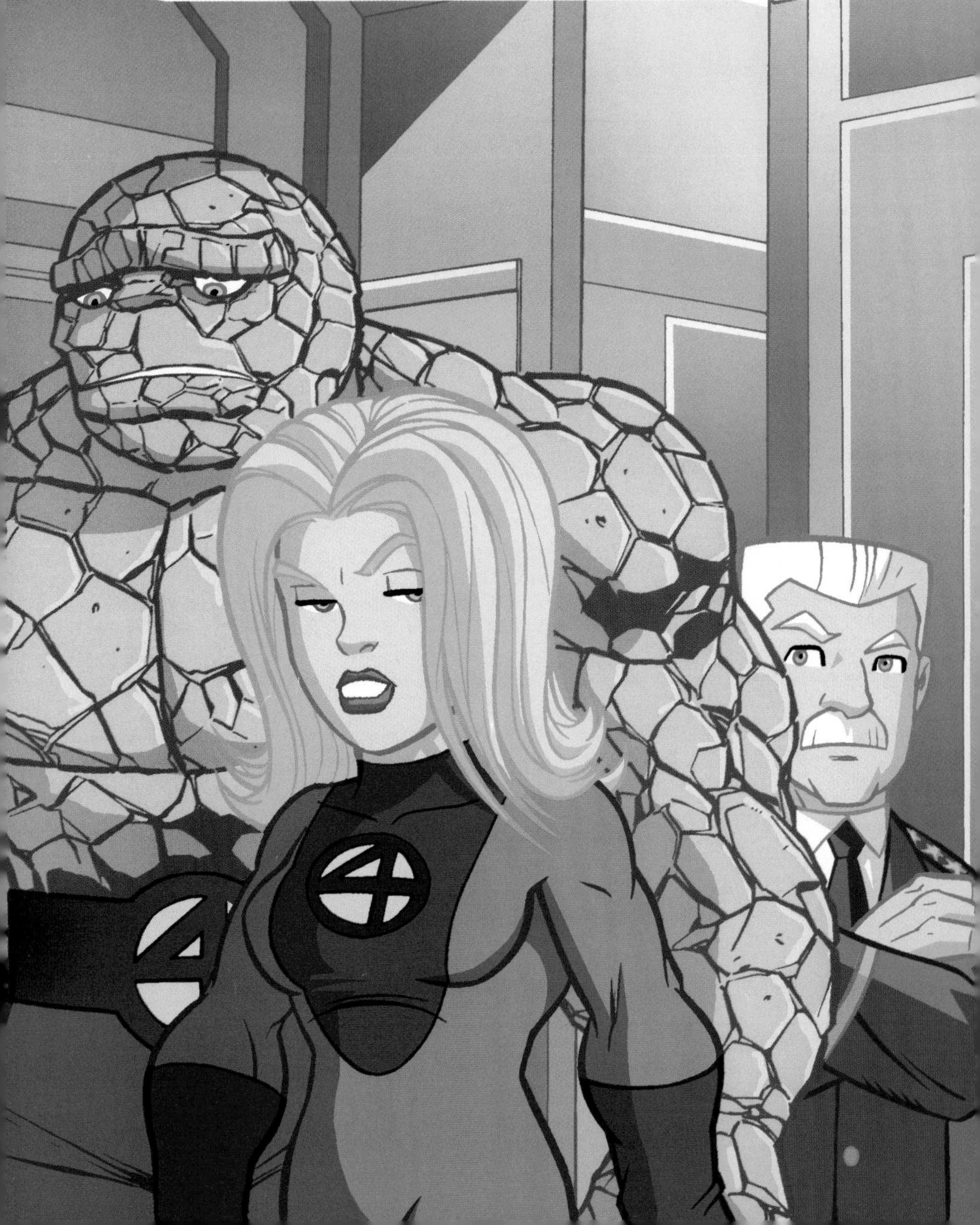

Wolverine hears what Thing
and Invisible Woman say.
He asks General Ross,
"What do they mean?"

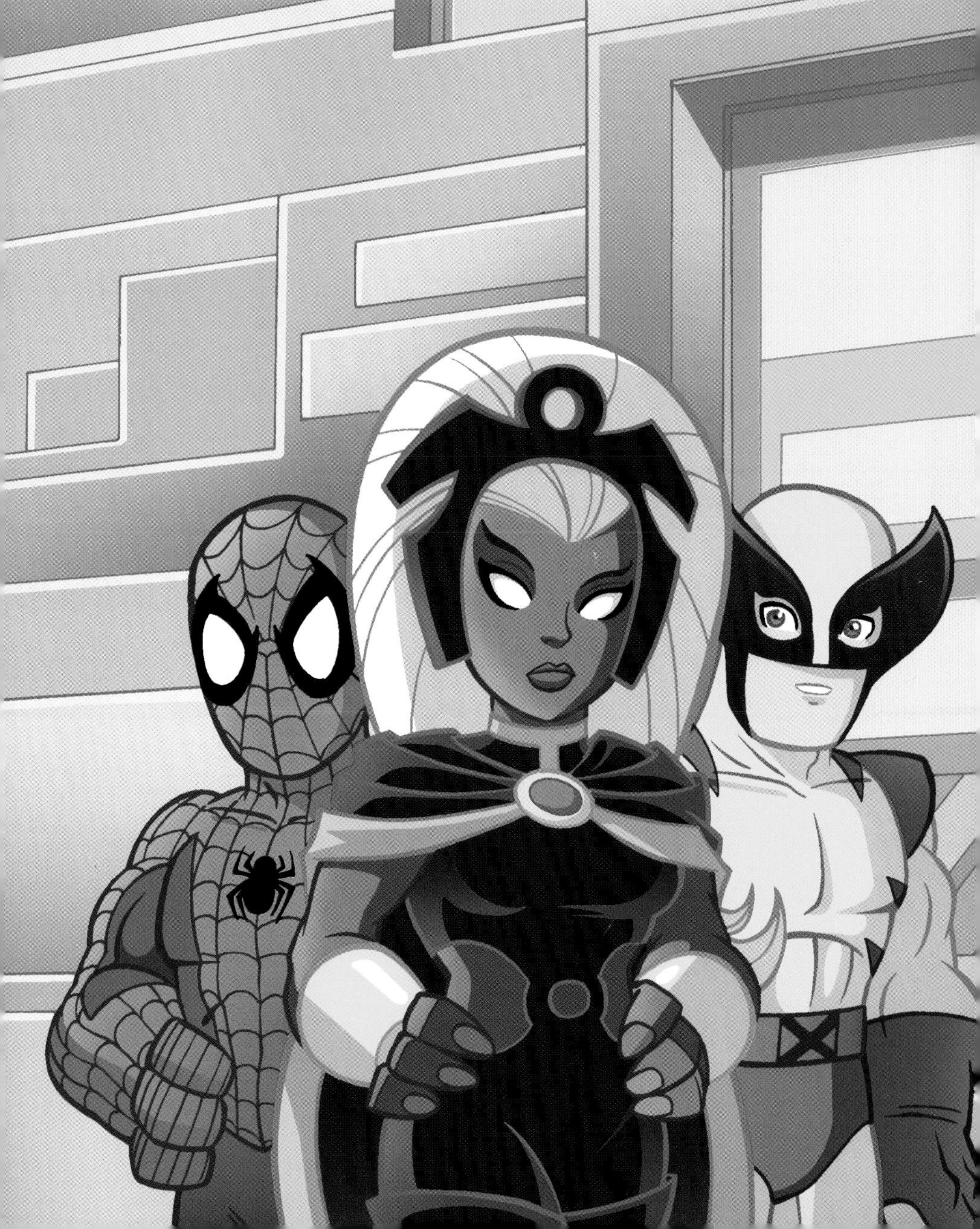

"You three do a great job," says Ross.
"But the other Squaddies
want to work with you, too."
"We like being a team," says Storm.
"We work so well together!"

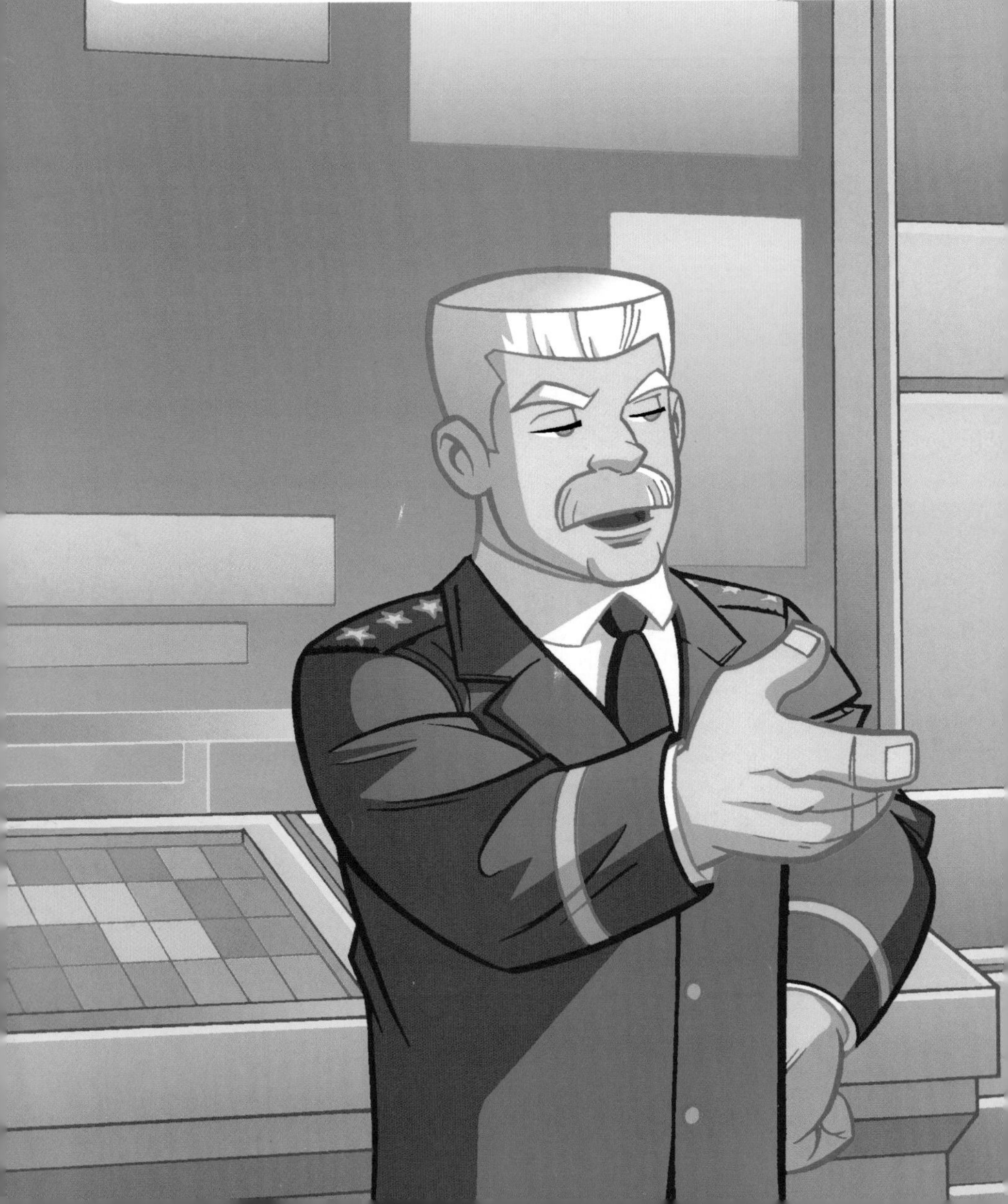

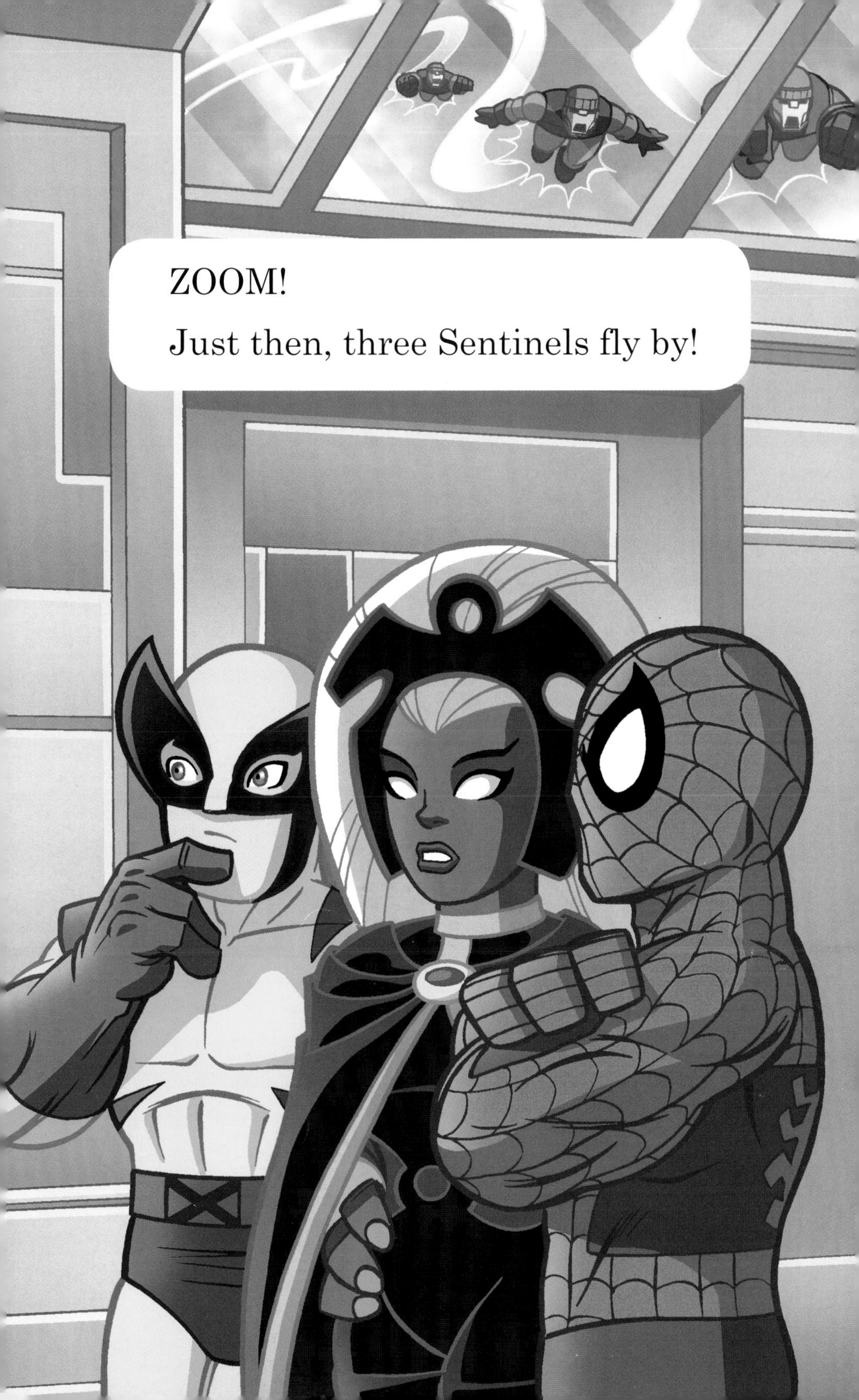

ZOOM!

Just then, three Sentinels fly by!

Dr. Doom appears on-screen.
“You cannot sneak into my lair
and get away with it!” he says, cackling.

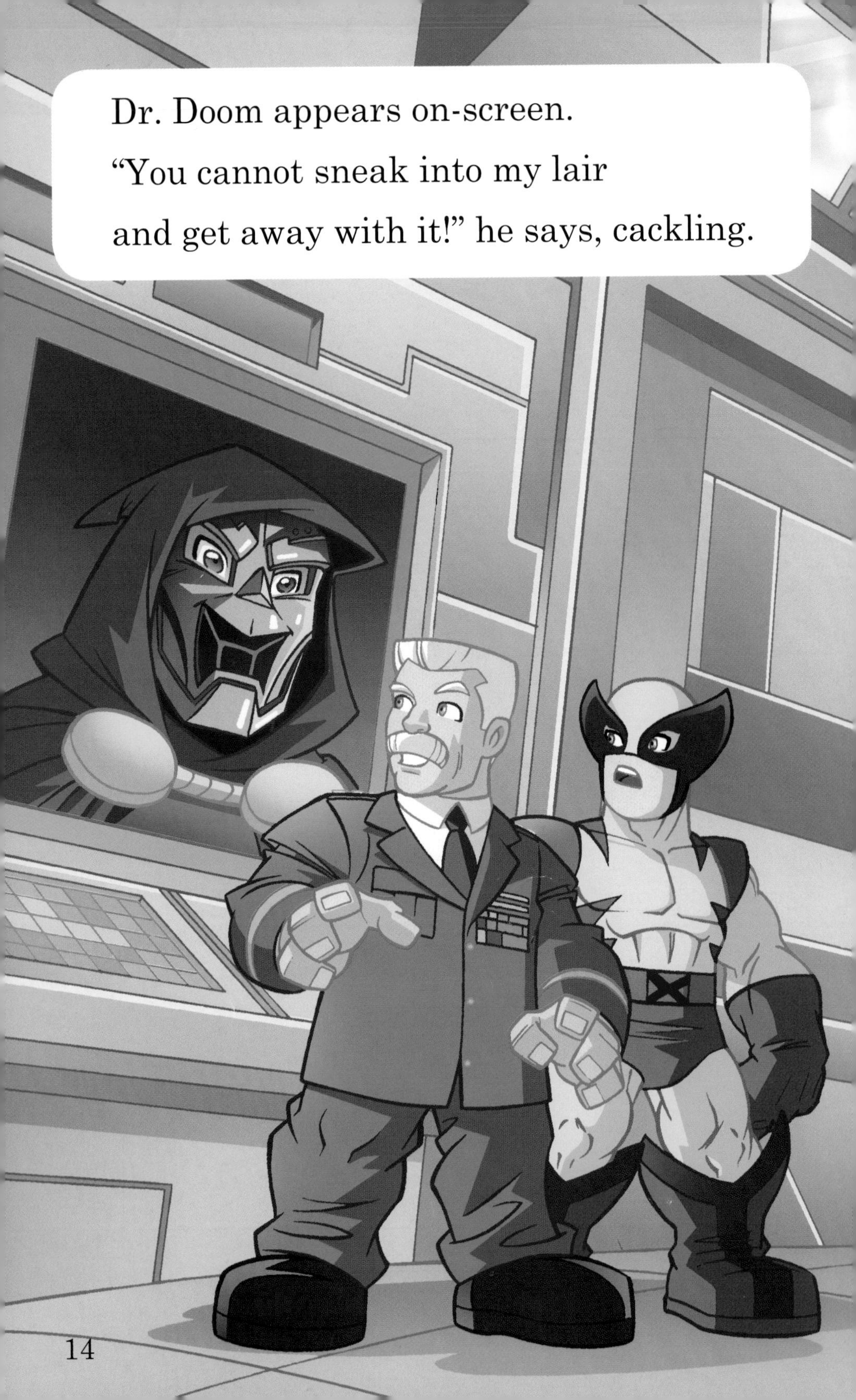

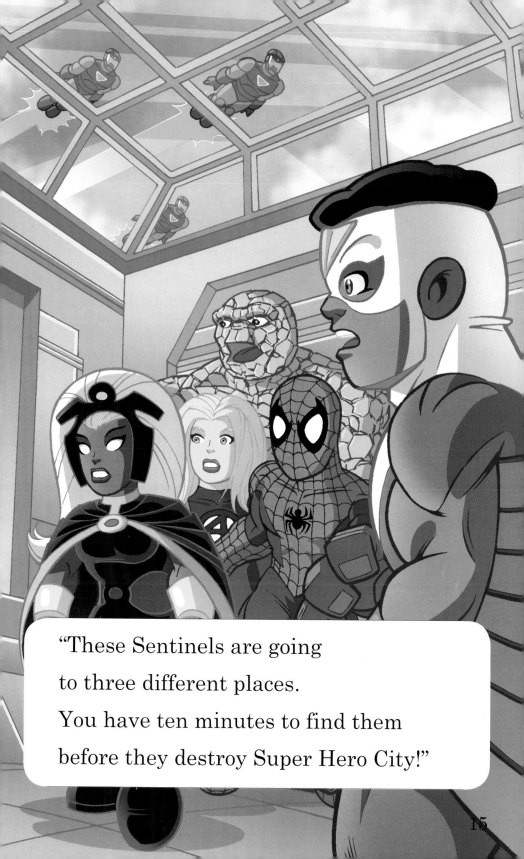

"These Sentinels are going
to three different places.
You have ten minutes to find them
before they destroy Super Hero City!"

“Squaddies, Hero Up!” cries General Ross.
“Spider-Man, team up with Falcon.
Wolverine, go with Invisible Woman.
Storm and Thing, work together.”

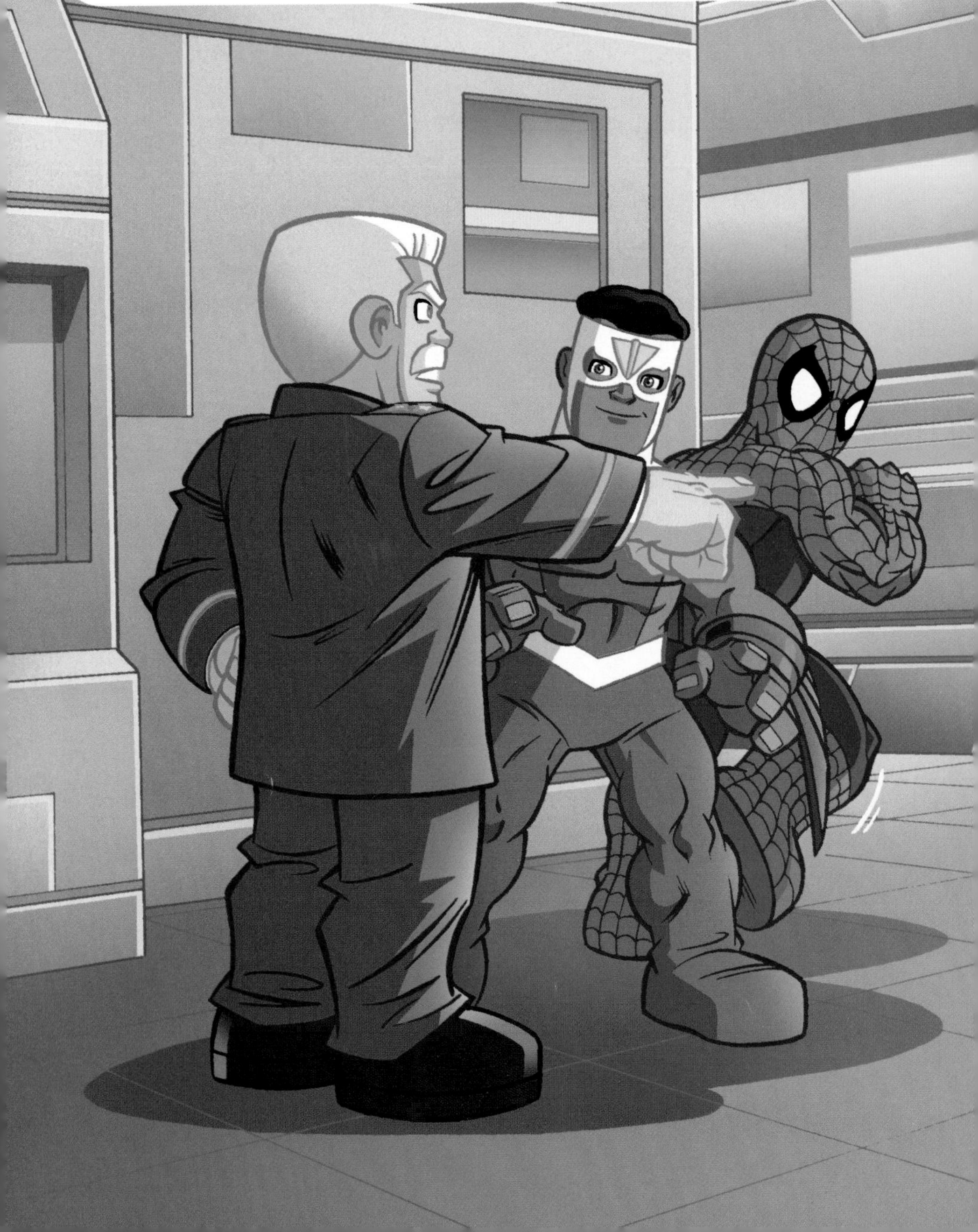

Wolverine, Spider-Man, and
Storm are not happy.
They want to work together.
But there is no time to argue.

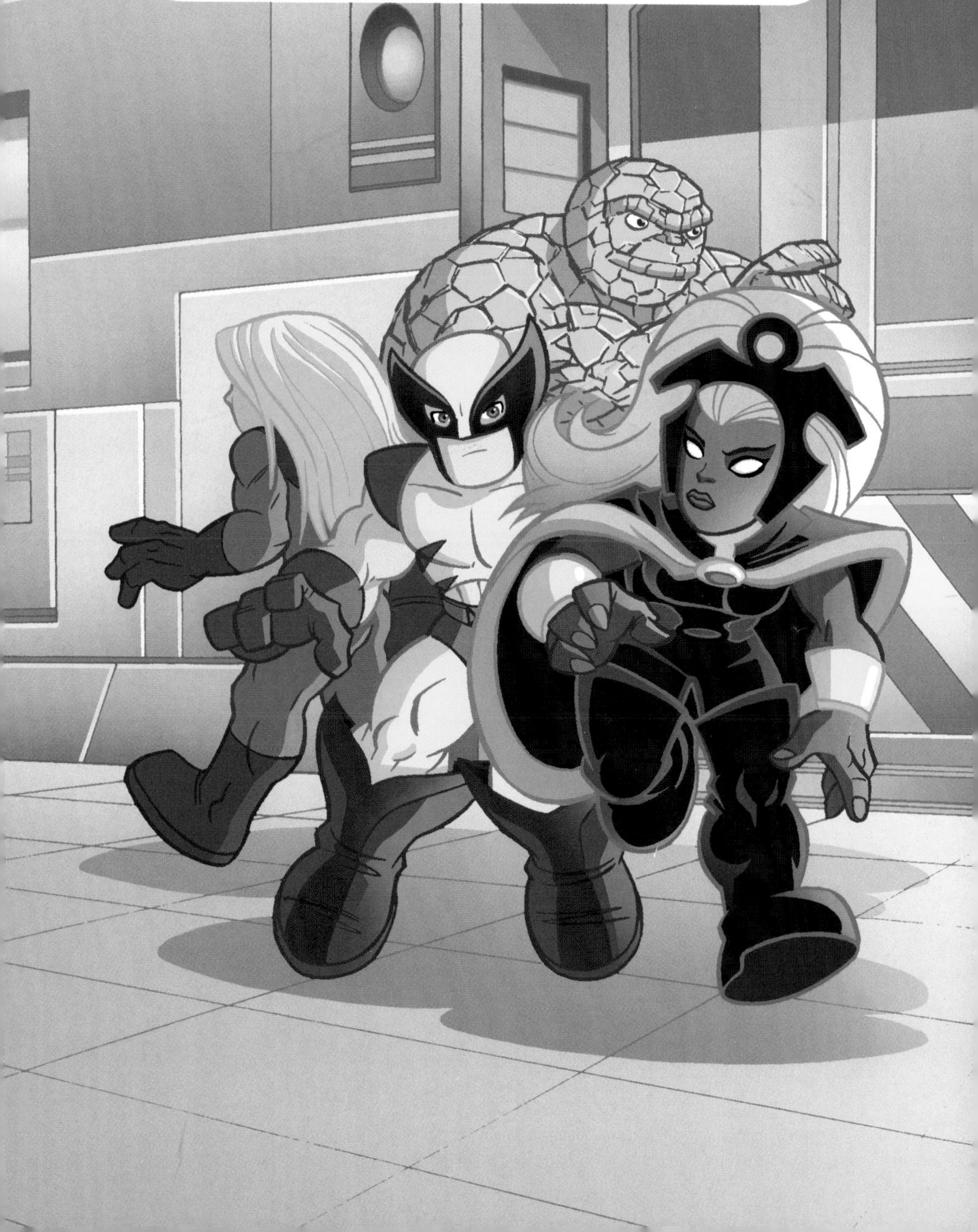

Spider-Man tries to think of a plan.
"Where did the Sentinels go?" he asks.
"I do not know where to start!"
"I do," says Falcon.

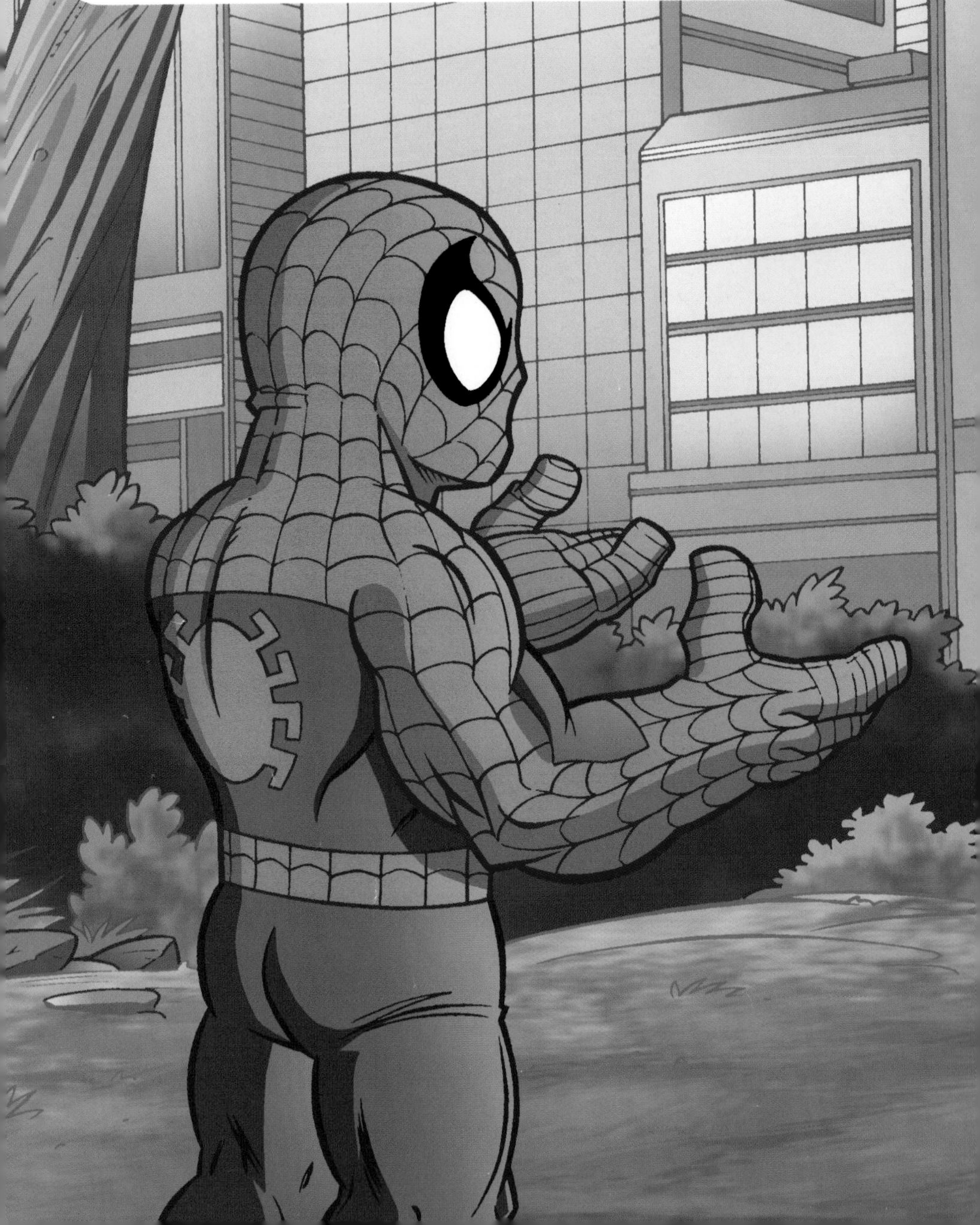

Falcon asks his bird friends
to help look for the Sentinels.
The birds of Super Hero City
tell the two Squaddies to go to City Hall.

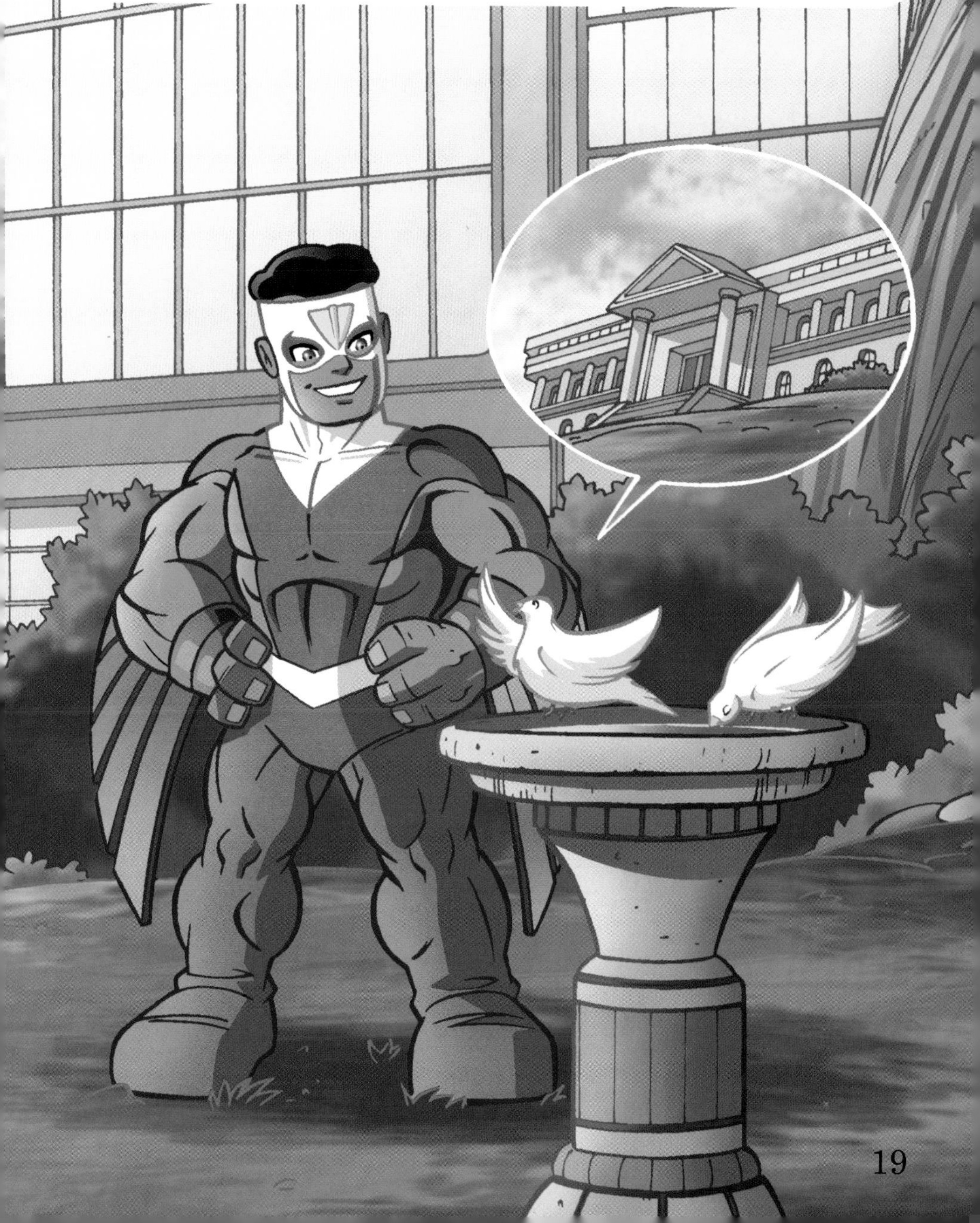

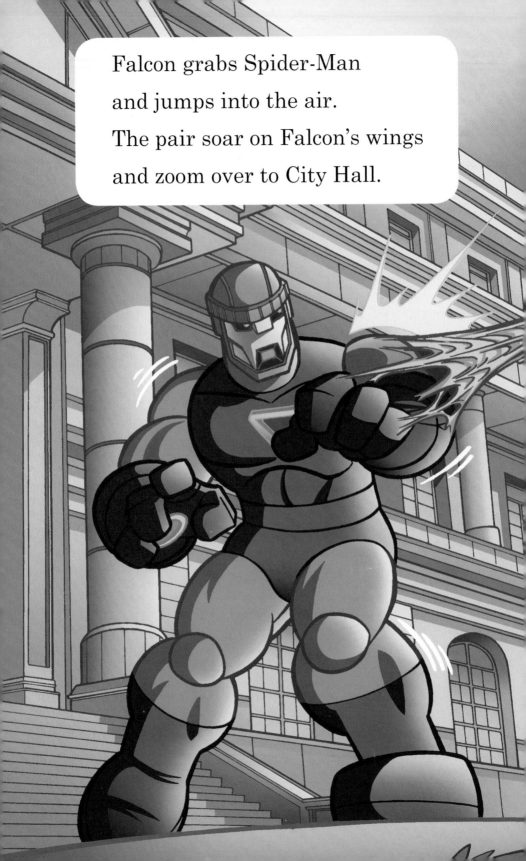

Falcon grabs Spider-Man
and jumps into the air.
The pair soar on Falcon's wings
and zoom over to City Hall.

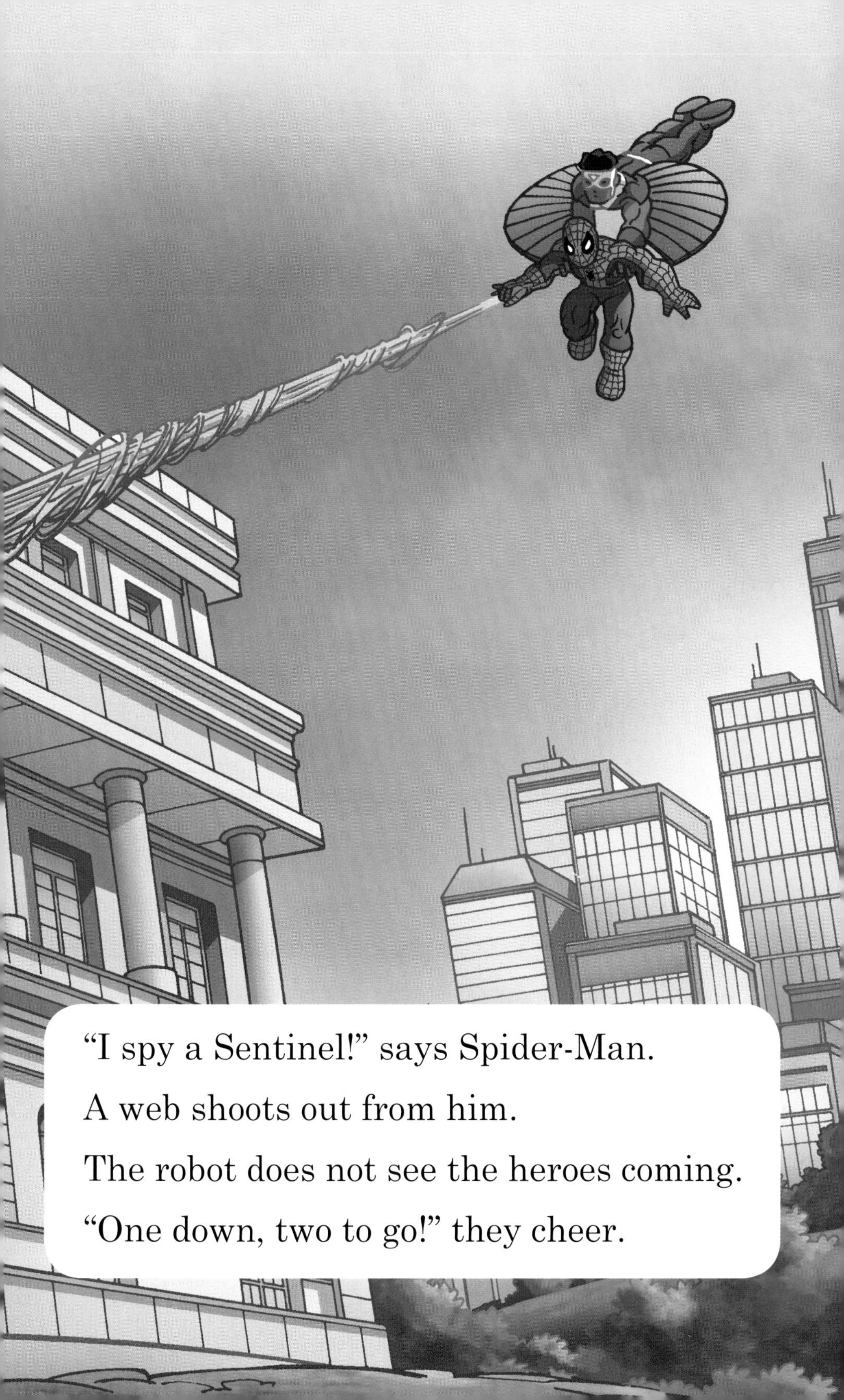

“I spy a Sentinel!” says Spider-Man.

A web shoots out from him.

The robot does not see the heroes coming.

“One down, two to go!” they cheer.

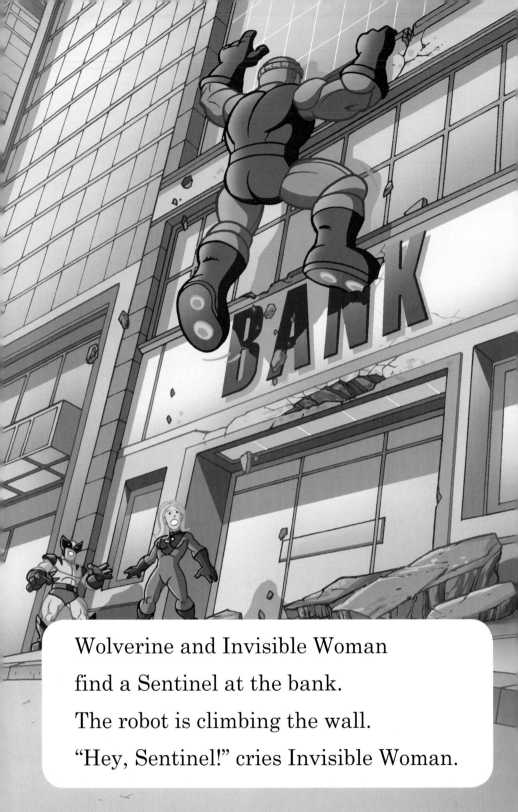

Wolverine and Invisible Woman
find a Sentinel at the bank.
The robot is climbing the wall.
"Hey, Sentinel!" cries Invisible Woman.

The Sentinel looks to its left,
and Invisible Woman disappears.
Then she reappears on the other side.
“I am right here!” she says, giggling.

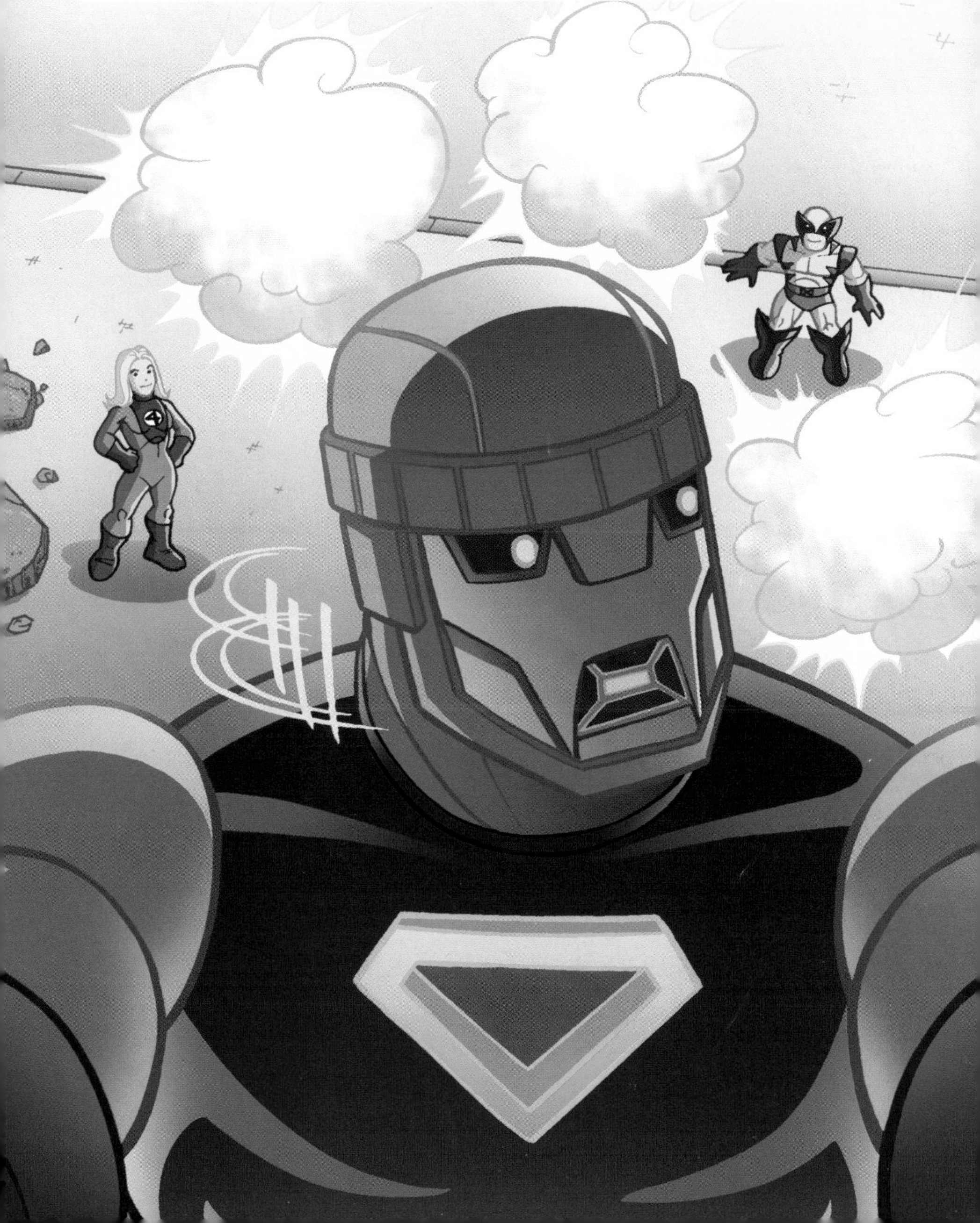

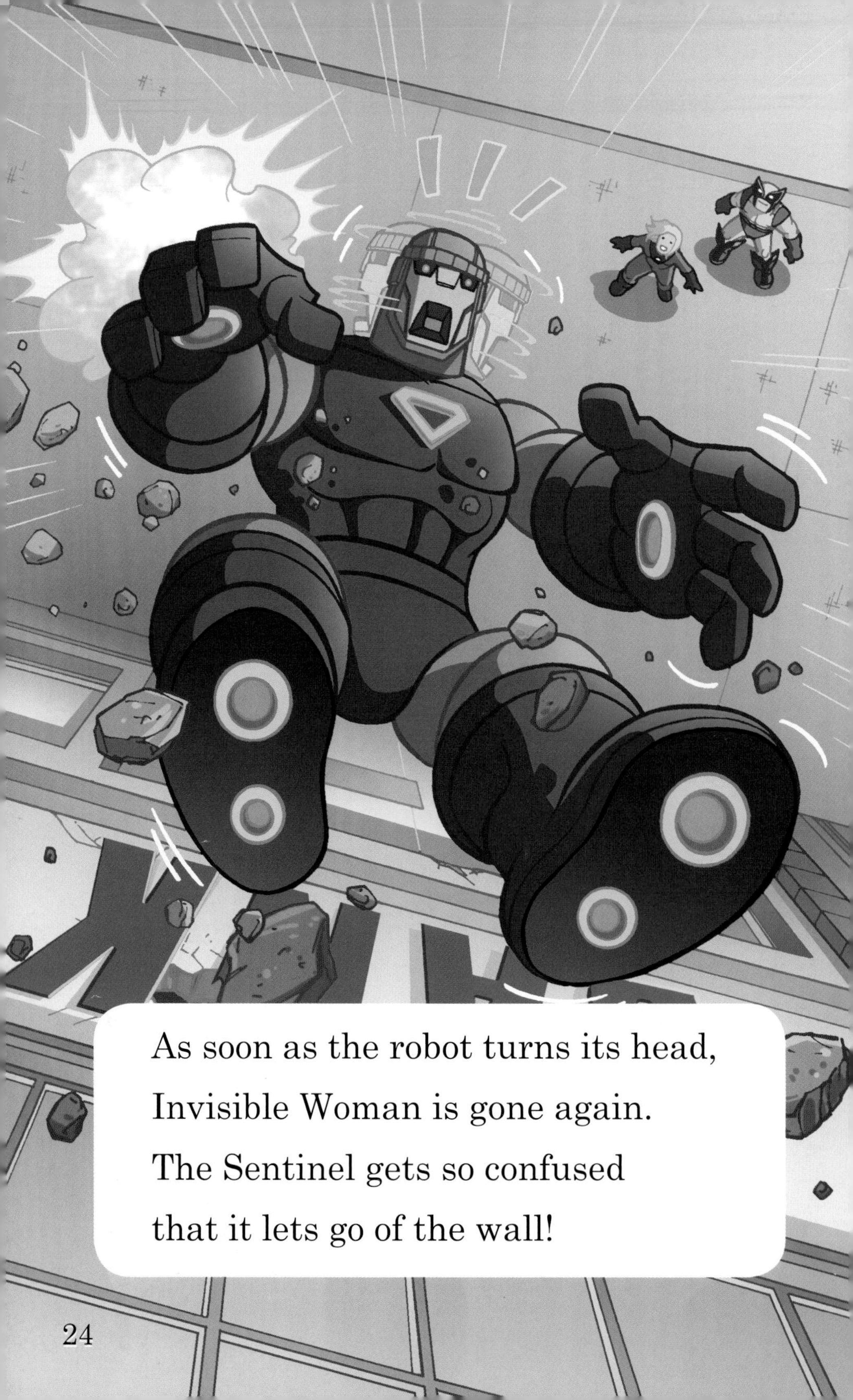

As soon as the robot turns its head,
Invisible Woman is gone again.
The Sentinel gets so confused
that it lets go of the wall!

The Sentinel crashes to the ground.
Wolverine leaps up to snip its wires.
"Nice job!" he says.
"Thanks!" says Invisible Woman.

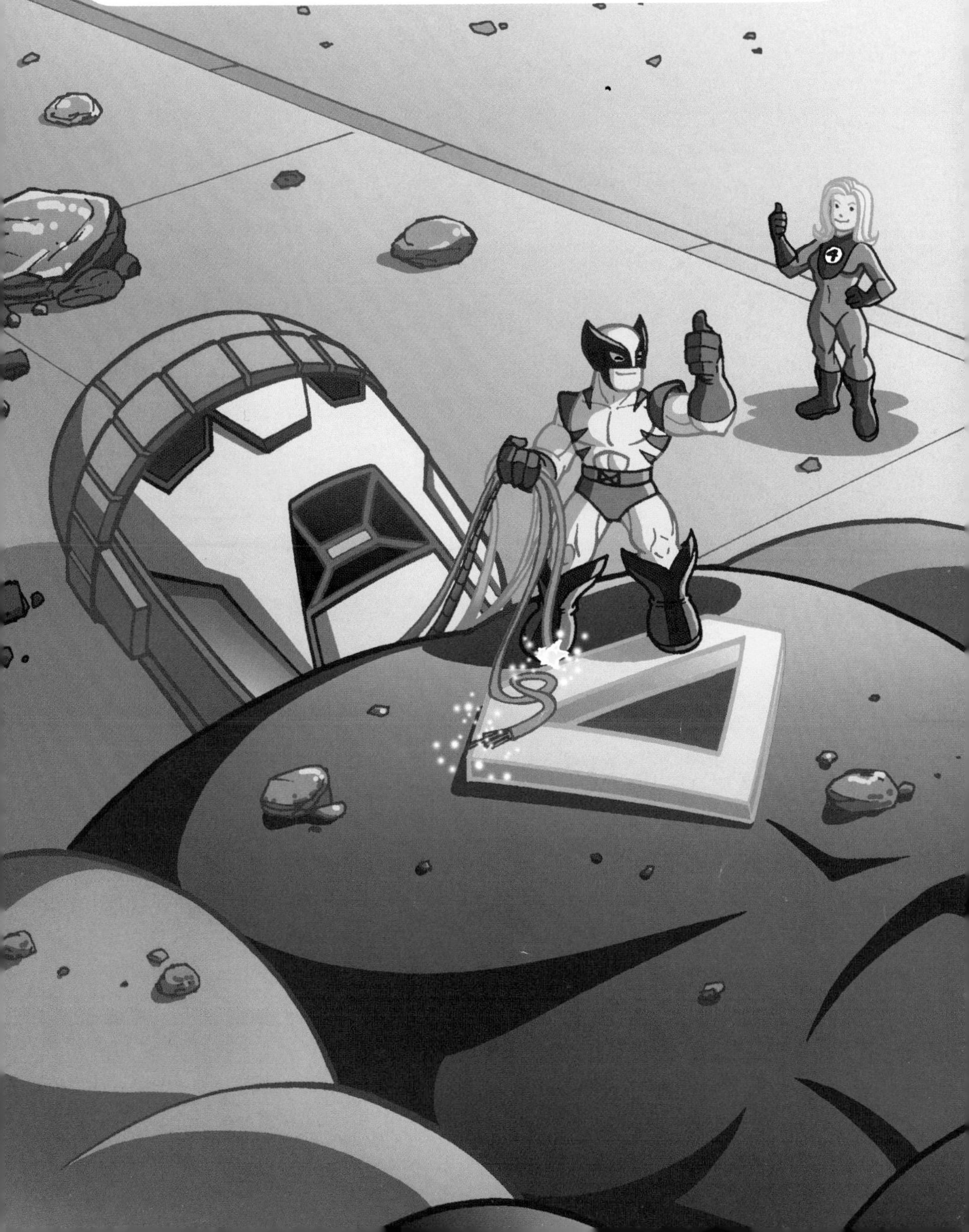

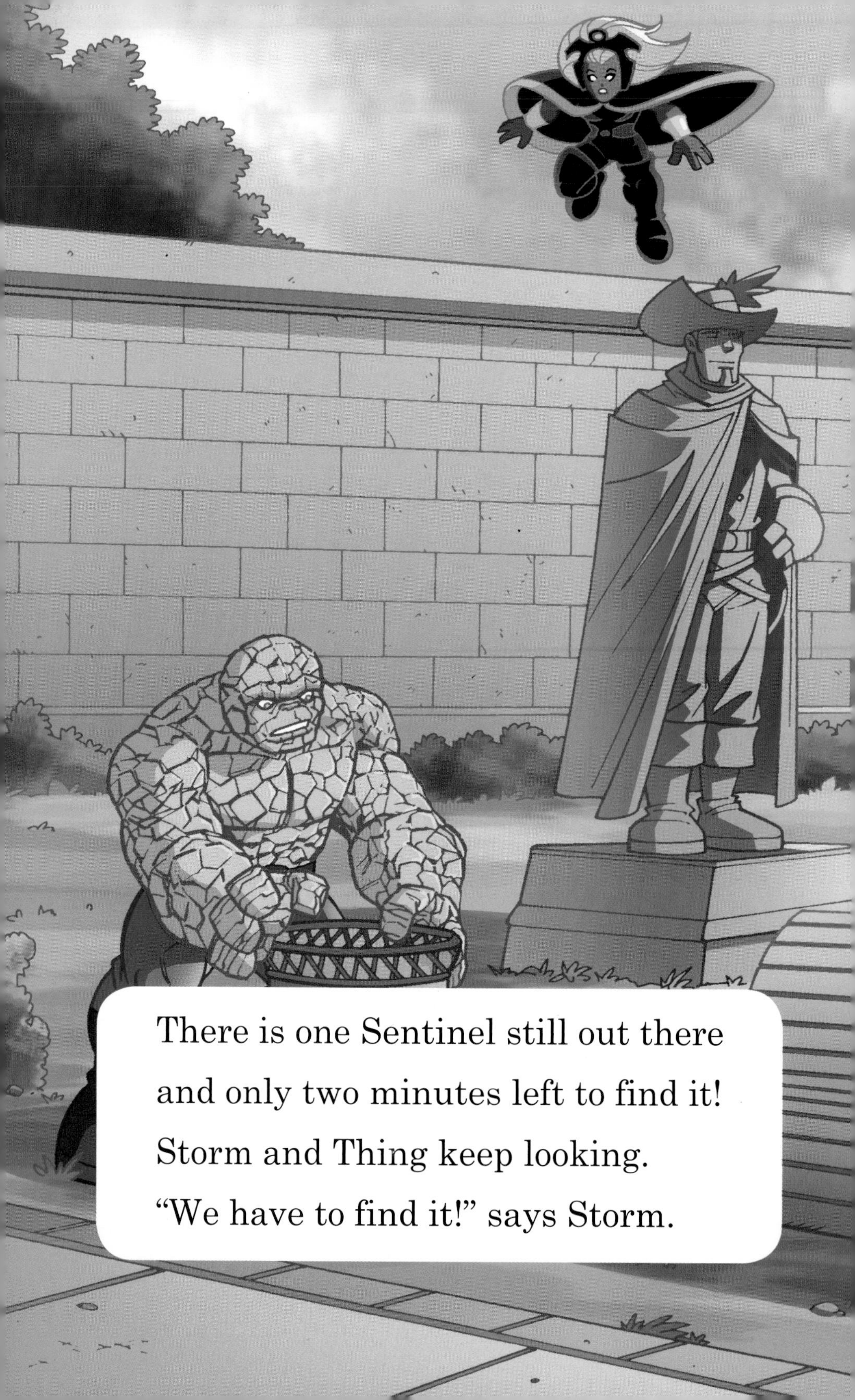

There is one Sentinel still out there
and only two minutes left to find it!
Storm and Thing keep looking.
“We have to find it!” says Storm.

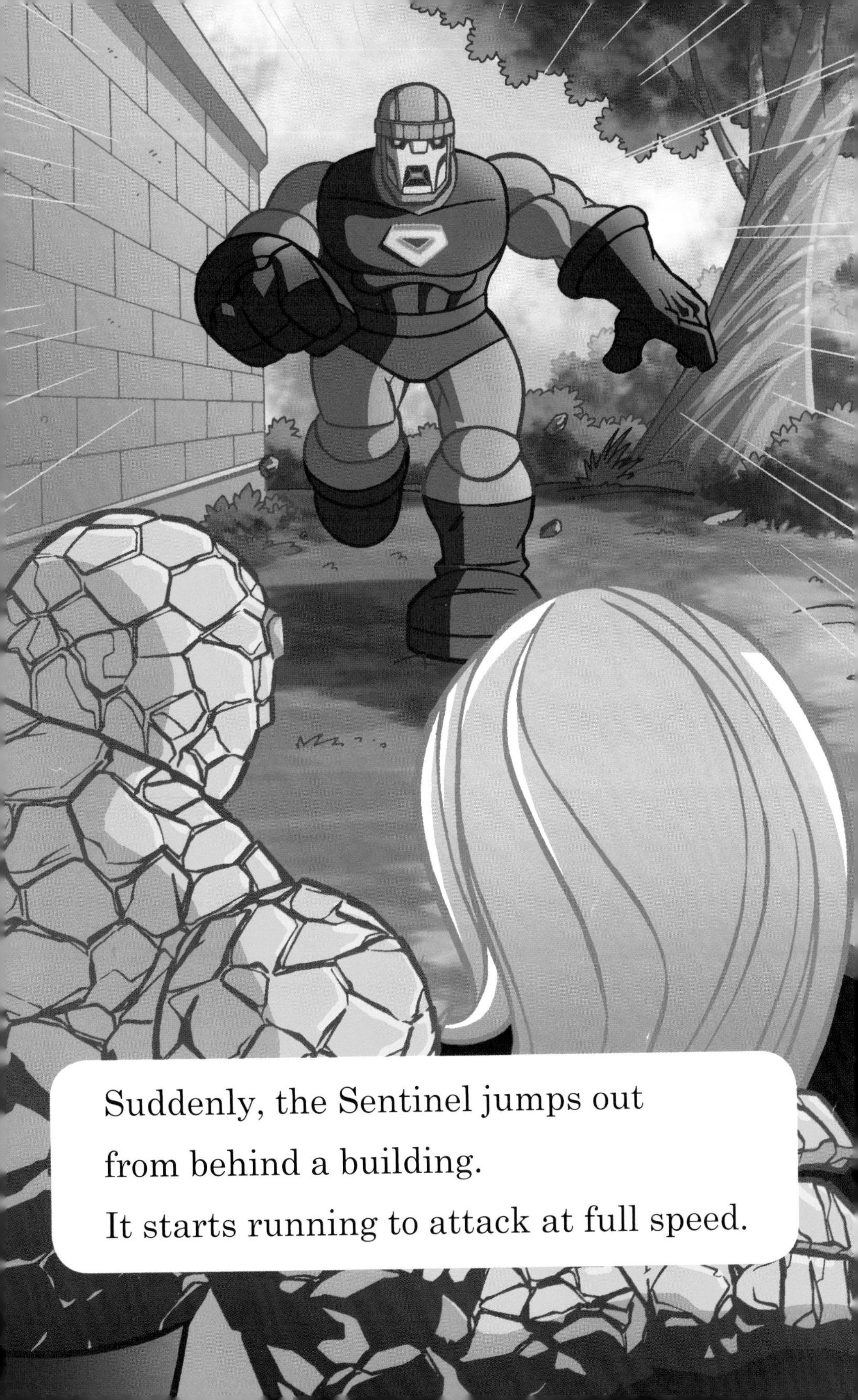

Suddenly, the Sentinel jumps out
from behind a building.
It starts running to attack at full speed.

"We need rain!" Thing calls out.
Storm uses her powers to make
drops of rain fall from the sky.
A huge mud puddle forms.

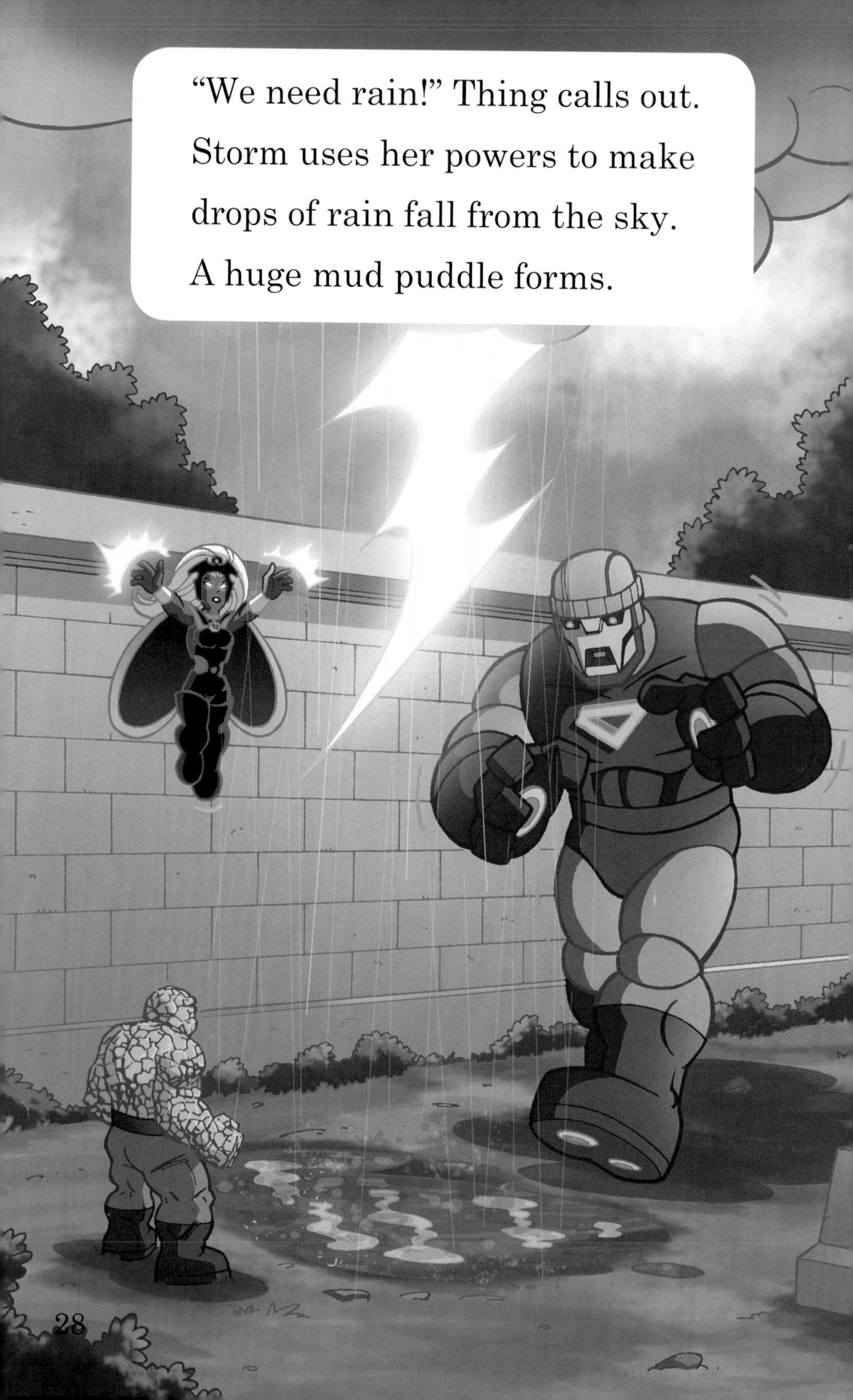

The robot slips in the mud and falls.
Thing smashes his fist into a statue.
It crumbles down around the robot.
The Sentinel is trapped!

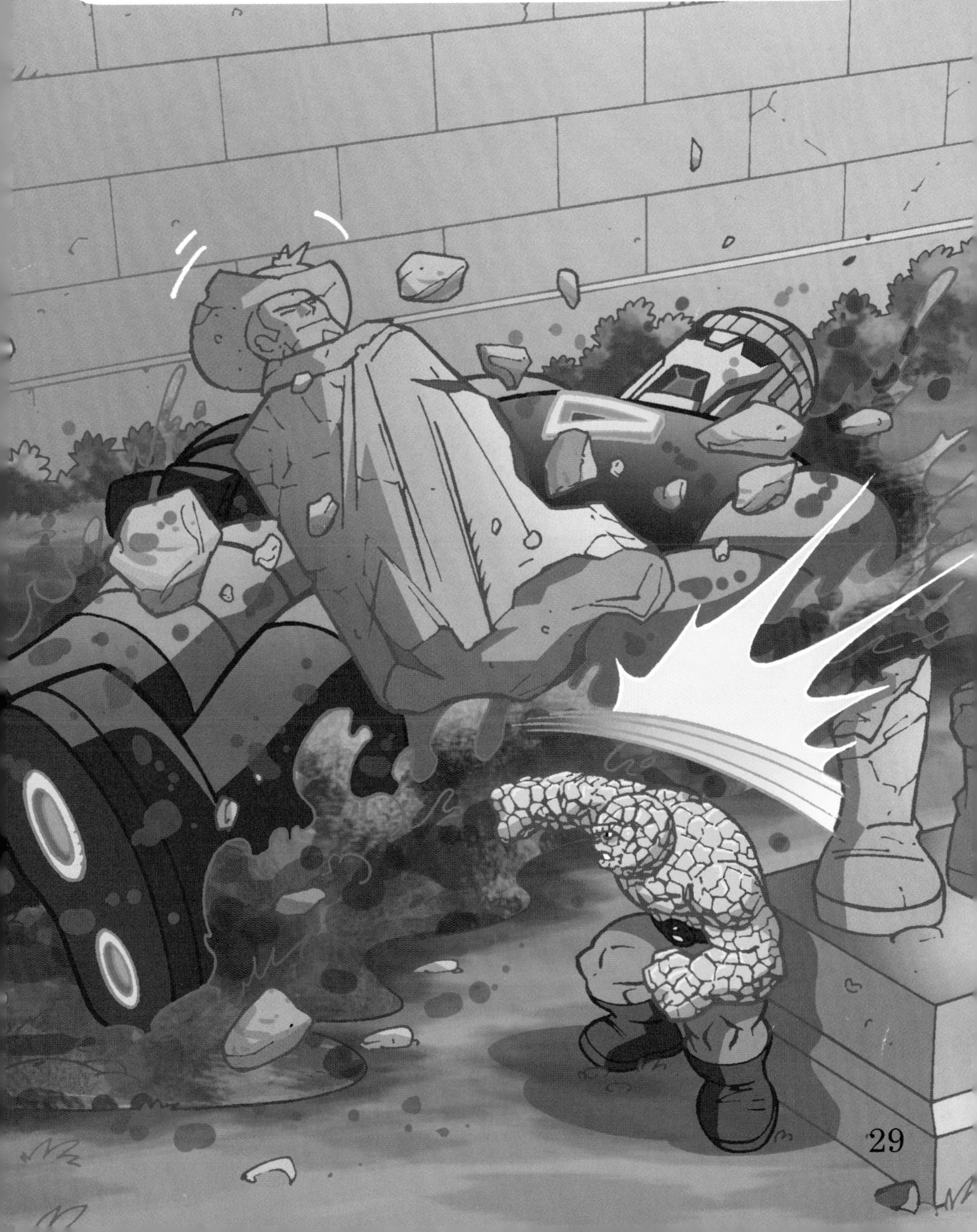

The Super Heroes tell General Ross
how they defeated all three Sentinels.
"Falcon was awesome," says Spider-Man.
"So was Invisible Woman," says Wolverine.
"So was Thing!" adds Storm.

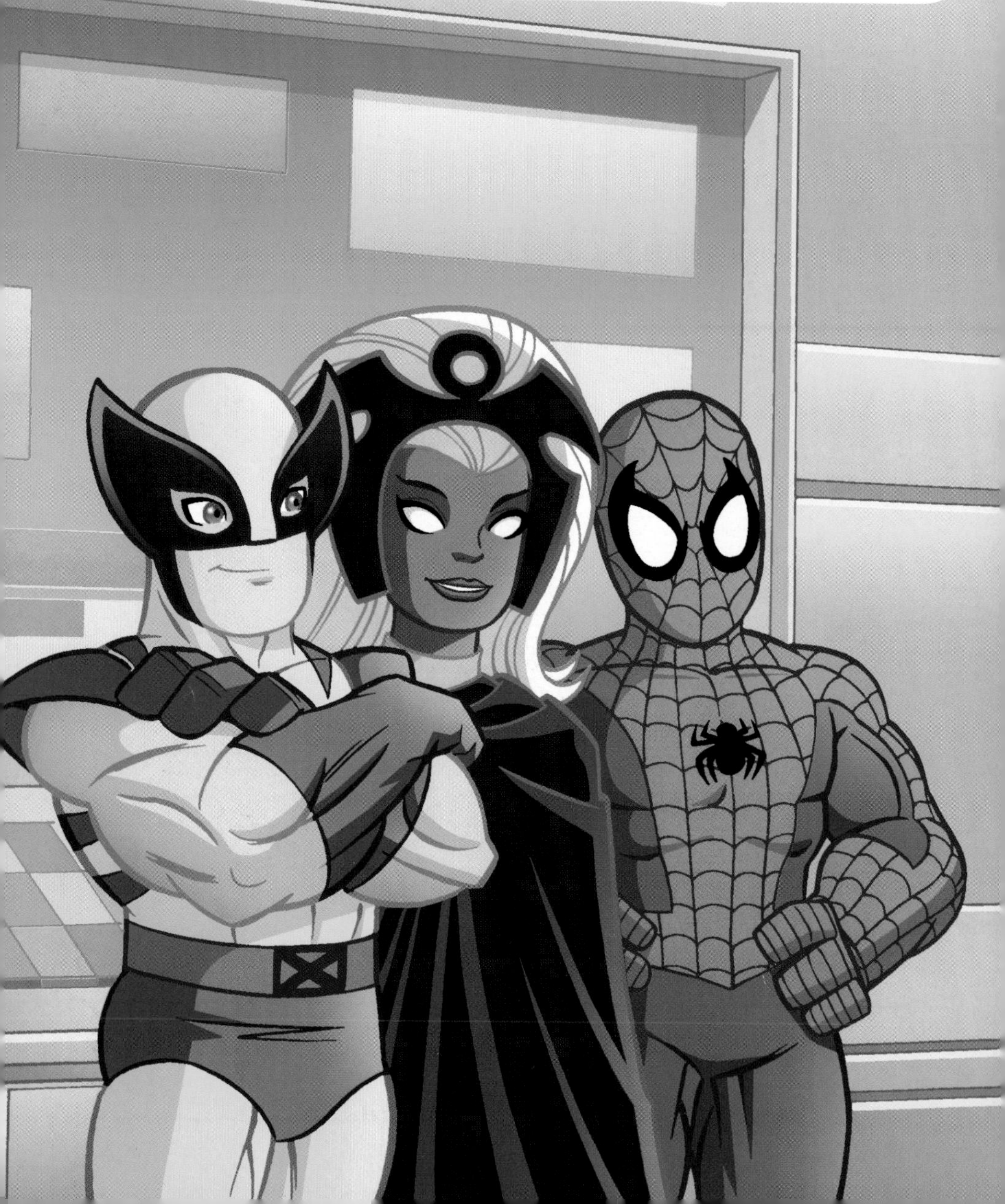

General Ross winks.

“Sorry to break you up,” he tells them.

“Do you want to be on one team again?”

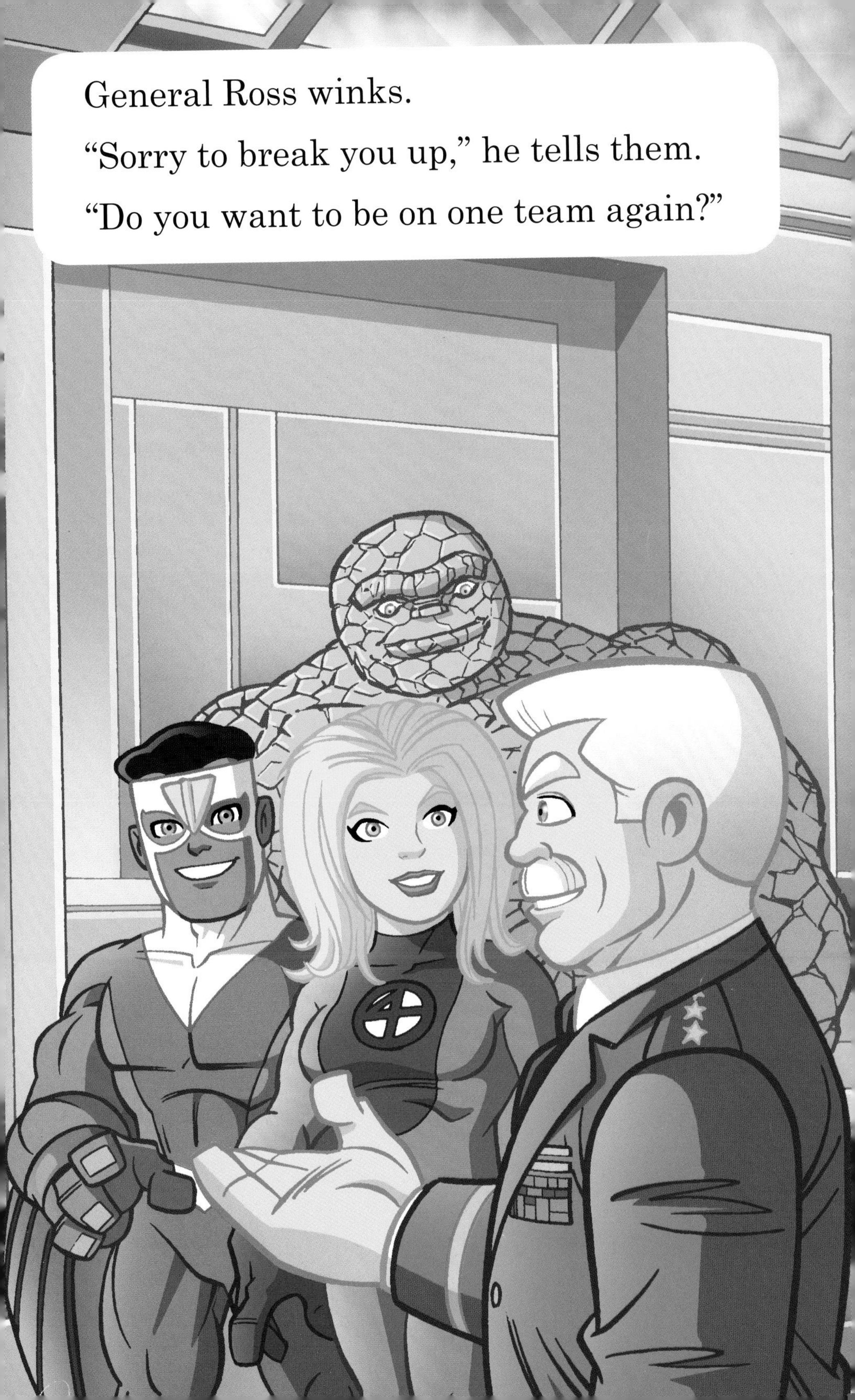

Spider-Man, Storm, and Wolverine smile.
"We *are* on one team," they say,
gathering all their friends.
"We are on the Super Hero Squad!"

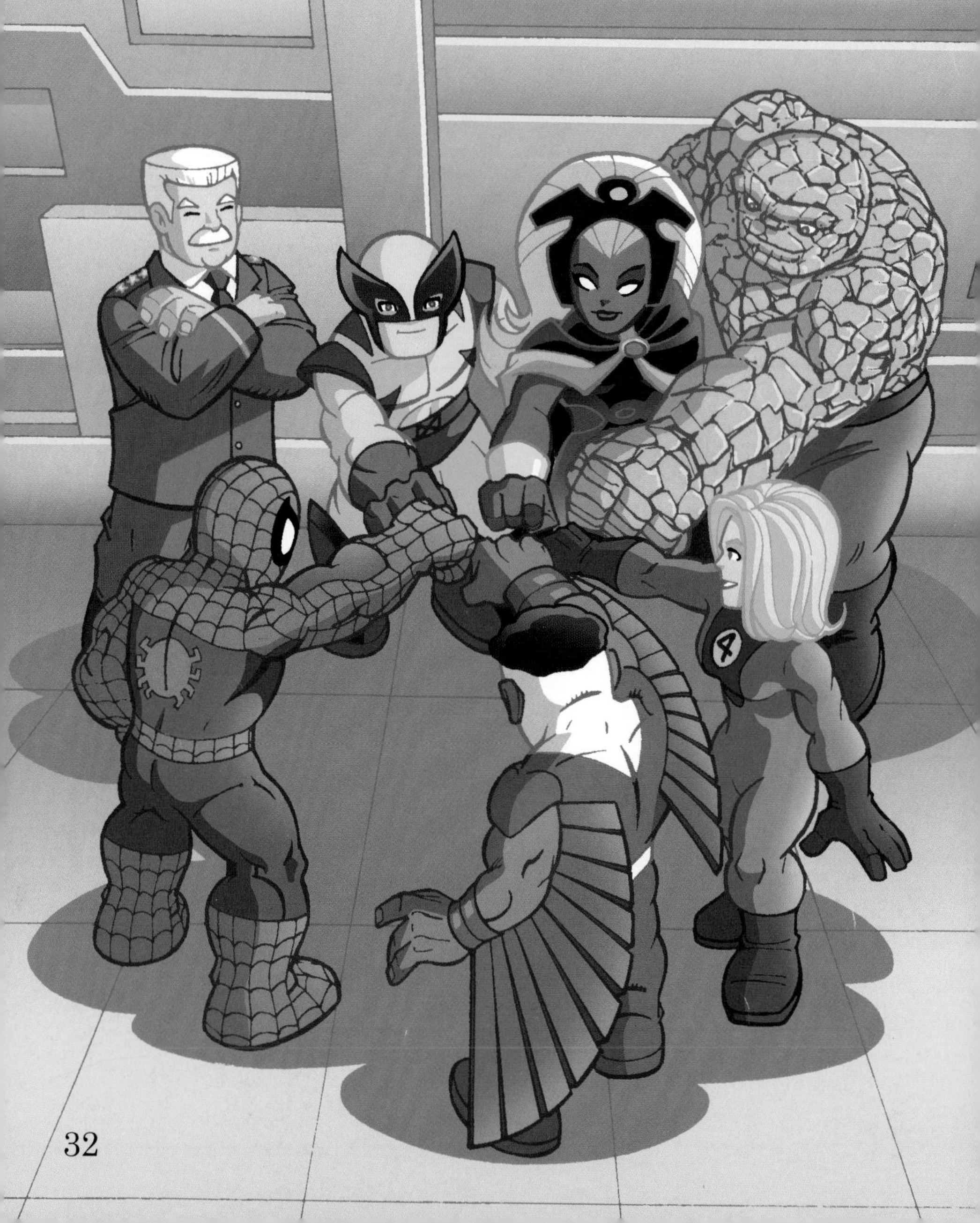